MICHAEL BOND

Paddington

HITS OUT

Illustrated by Barry Wilkinson

COLLINS COLOUR CUBS

One day Mr. Curry decided to enter a golf competition, and he asked Paddington to be his caddy.

"All you have to do, bear, is look after my clubs," he boomed.

Paddington wasn't very keen on doing things for the Browns' neighbour. They always seemed to go wrong. All the same, he felt most important as he took Mr. Curry's bag.

"I do hope he'll be all right," said Mrs. Brown anxiously, as Paddington set off next day. "You know how bad-tempered Mr. Curry gets, and golf isn't the easiest of games."

Mrs. Bird gave a snort. As far as she was concerned Mr. Curry deserved all he got. "He's for ever trying to get something for nothing," she said.

All the same, she began to look slightly worried as she waved goodbye. With Paddington let loose on a golf course there was no knowing what might happen.

ARNOLD PARKER

GOLF
COMPETITION

By the time Paddington reached the golf
club quite a large crowd had already
collected, and several of them applauded
as he made his way towards the first hole.

Paddington decided he liked golf courses and he raised his hat politely in return.

Even Arnold Parker, the world-famous golf champion, who was acting as judge, gave him a friendly salute.

"Good afternoon, Mr. Parker," called Paddington, returning the wave as he hurried on his way.

Mr. Curry was already waiting impatiently for him.

"Ah, there you are, bear," he growled. "I thought you were never coming."

"Now this is a very important part of the competition," he continued. "It's to see who can hit their ball the farthest. There's a special prize for the winner so I want you to make sure my ball doesn't get lost."

"Don't worry, Mr. Curry," said Paddington. "I've marked it with a special marmalade chunk. Look . . ."

"Are you sure it won't come off, bear?" growled Mr. Curry.

"*Quite* sure," said Paddington firmly, as he took up the position he'd seen Arnold Parker use. "Mrs. Bird says my chunks stick to anything."

"Hm. Well, I hope you're right, bear,"
growled Mr. Curry. "If you're not . . ."
He broke off as a loud cracking noise came
from Paddington's direction.

"Bear!" he bellowed. "That's my best club you've broken! How dare you! Wait until we get back. You won't hear the last of this!"

"Perhaps you could tie the two ends together, Mr. Curry?" said Paddington hopefully.

"Tie the two ends together!" spluttered Mr. Curry. "Why . . . I've . . ." He broke off as he caught sight of someone coming their way.

"Well?" he demanded. "What do *you* want?"

Paddington jumped to his feet. "Hello, Mr. Parker," he exclaimed. "I'm afraid I've been having trouble with one of Mr. Curry's clubs!"

"Oh, dear," said Arnold Parker. "You're welcome to borrow mine if you like."

"Parker," exclaimed Mr. Curry. "Not *the* Arnold Parker? I had no idea you two knew each other. You didn't tell me, bear.

"Of course, I was only joking just now," he continued, rubbing his hands in invisible soap.

"Remind me to give you five pence when we get home!

"Any friend of yours, bear, is a friend of mine," said Mr. Curry.

"Now, have you got my tee?"

"Your tea, Mr. Curry?"

Anxious to make amends while the Browns' neighbour was in a good mood, Paddington peered in the bag, but it seemed to be empty.

"You can have a marmalade sandwich
if you like," he announced, removing a
shapeless white object from inside his
hat. "I brought it in case I had an
emergency."

"Bah!" snorted Mr. Curry, his bad temper getting the better of him again. "I don't mean the sort of tea you eat ... I want it to put my ball on so that I can address it."

Paddington began to look more and more confused. He'd never heard of anyone hitting a ball off a marmalade sandwich before, let alone writing their address on it.

Arnold Parker gave a cough. "I think," he said, handing Mr. Curry a small yellow object, "your friend wants one of these. It's what we golfers call a tee. It's to stand your ball on. When we get ready to hit it we say we're addressing it."

It seemed to Paddington a very compli-
cated way to go about hitting a small ball
with a piece of metal on the end of a stick.

All the same, as Mr. Curry lifted his club and Arnold Parker hissed a word of warning, he did as he was told and hurried off to take cover behind a nearby sand dune.

But he'd barely gone a couple of steps when he was stopped dead in his tracks by a loud cry from Mr. Curry. And when he looked round he saw why.

Mr. Curry appeared to be turning a cartwheel.

"Oh, dear," said Arnold Parker. "I think you've trodden on your friend's marmalade sandwich."

"Bah!" bellowed Mr. Curry. "I've hurt my leg. Now I shan't be able to play. It's all your fault, bear!"

"Perhaps," said Paddington, "I could do it for you, Mr. Curry. Bears are good at hitting things. Besides, your club is just the right length now."

"A good idea," said Arnold Parker. "There's nothing in the rules to say bears can't take part in the competition. Why not?"

Mr. Curry gazed at Paddington, then at the ball, still lying where he'd placed it.

He looked as if he could have thought
of a good many reasons why not, but the
rattle of an approaching goods train
made him change his mind.

"All right, bear," he growled. "But
watch what you're doing."

Paddington needed no second bidding. Before Mr. Curry had time to change his mind, he'd taken careful aim and with a satisfying clunk the ball went sailing into the air.

"Fore!" shouted Arnold Parker, above the roar of the train.

"Five!" cried Paddington excitedly.

He'd never hit a golf ball before and although it hadn't quite gone in the direction he'd intended, he could hardly believe his good fortune at doing so well.

"Congratulations!" said Arnold Parker
as he picked himself up. "Did anyone
see where it went?"

"I did," bellowed Mr. Curry. "It went over there . . . towards the railway line. And if it's been run over by that train . . . I'll . . . I'll . . ."

Paddington never did learn what Mr. Curry would have done had his golf ball been run over, for as luck would have it something very strange happened. Something even Mr. Curry couldn't grumble at . . .

. . . especially when he found himself being presented with a brand new set of golf clubs later that day.

"Do you mean to say I've won these?" he exclaimed.

"No," said Mrs. Bird. "*Paddington* did, but he's giving them to you to make up for breaking yours."

"Your ball went nine miles," said Judy proudly.

"Arnold Parker says it must be a world record," added Jonathan. "I bet the engine driver was surprised."

"*Nine* miles?" repeated Mr. Curry. "*Engine* driver? What *are* you talking about?"

"Your ball landed in that goods train by mistake, Mr. Curry," explained Paddington. "The driver sent it back from the next station, and Mr. Parker said there was nothing in the rules to stop it being counted. So I won first prize."

"Bears," said Mrs. Bird, "always fall on their feet."

"That's what Mr. Parker said," agreed Paddington. "He's going to put marmalade chunks on *all* his golf balls in future . . . just like this one. He thinks it might bring him luck.

"I should do the same to yours, Mr.
Curry. Besides, if you ever get lost in a
bunker at least you won't go hungry."

This story comes from PADDINGTON GOES TO TOWN
and is based on the television film. It has been
specially written by Michael Bond for
younger children.

ISBN 0 00 123206 1 (paperback)
ISBN 0 00 123213 4 (cased)
Text copyright © 1977 Michael Bond
Illustrations copyright © 1977 William Collins Sons & Co. Ltd.
Cover copyright © 1977 William Collins Sons & Co. Ltd. and Film Fair Ltd.
Cover design by Ivor Wood. Cover photographed by Bruce Scott.
Printed in Great Britain